To Kian, Rayan, and Luke

Dial Books for Young Readers
Penguin Young Readers Group
An imprint of Penguin Random House LLC
375 Hudson Street, New York, NY 10014

Library of Congress Cataloging-in-Publication Data
Names: Agee, Jon, author, illustrator.
Title: Lion lessons / Jon Agee.
Description: New York, NY : Dial Books for Young Readers, [2016] | Summary:
  "Learning to be a lion takes some serious lessons, but luckily, this kid
   has a teacher who is a real pro"— Provided by publisher.
Identifiers: LCCN 2015022743 | ISBN 9780803739086 (hardcover)
Subjects: | CYAC: Lions—Fiction.
Classification: LCC PZ7.A266 Lg 2016 | DDC [E]—dc23
LC record available at http://lccn.loc.gov/2015022743

Printed in China • Design by Lily Malcom • Text set in ITC Charter

10 9 8 7 6 5 4 3 2 1

It's not easy getting your Lion Diploma.
I know. I took lessons.

My teacher was a pro.
"There are seven steps to becoming a lion," he said.
"But first we must stretch!"

We did the Upward Lion,

the Downward Lion,

the Upside-Down Lion,

the Rolling Lion,

the Flying Lion,

and we shook
our manes.

Step One was Looking Fierce.
"Watch me," said the lion. "You bare your claws,
gnash your teeth, and show your fangs."

I tried out my three most frightening poses.
The lion wasn't impressed.

Step Two was Roaring.

"It's simple," said the lion. "Take a deep breath
and roar as loud as you can into the microphone."

I took a deep breath and roared as loud as I could.
"Needs work," said the lion.

Step Three was Choosing What to Eat.
The lion showed me the menu.

"Are there any specials?" I asked. "You know, like, spaghetti?"
The lion growled. "We don't eat spaghetti!"

Step Four was Prowling Around.
We crept through the woods,
trying to be invisible.

We hid in the bushes.
"I can see your tail," said the lion.

We hid behind trees.
"Your tail," said the lion. "I can still see it."

Step Five was Sprinting.
"Do you see that tree?" said the lion.
I looked around.
"You mean the little one here?"
"No," said the lion. "The big one on that faraway hill.
I'll meet you there in five minutes."

It took me an hour.
"You need to hit the gym," said the lion.

Step Six was Pouncing.

"It's simple," said the lion. "You get a running start
and then you jump on that lady."

"But I'll scare her to death!"

"Uh, that's the idea," said the lion.

So, I got a running start—

—and I pounced.

"What a cute little kitty-cat!"
said the lady. "Are you lost?"
"Meow," I said.

The lion checked my scores.
"This is not very promising."

Step Seven was Looking Out for Your Friends.

Right away, I spotted a kitten.
"Friend or foe?" said the lion.
"That's easy," I said. "Friend."

"What about that dog?"

I let out a ferocious roar.

I bared my claws, gnashed my teeth, pawed the ground, shook my mane, and then . . .

I sprinted across the field as fast as I could—

AND POUNCED!

Exactly like a—
well, you know—
a LION!

"Bravo!" said the lion.

And that's how I got my diploma.

I'm very proud of it . . .

but now the neighborhood cats won't leave me alone!